Flash Horror

Susan O'Reilly

Published by Susan O'Reilly, 2023.

FLASH HORROR

First edition. February 25, 2023.

Copyright © 2023 Susan O'Reilly.

ISBN: 979-8215188170

Written by Susan O'Reilly.

Also by Susan O'Reilly

Changes Come
Snapshots
The Sound of Silence
Obsession a Novella Extended to Novel
Flash Horror

Star of the Show

Blood and guts stream across the screen. I laugh uproariously. The only thing scary about this movie is the looks I'm getting from the couple in front. They need to get a life. I mean, seriously, her hiding her head in his shoulder is a sure sign of the first date - make him feel brave and strong, a load of crap.

I've long since stopped going to movies for anything to do with romantic notions. I like to immerse myself into the cinema screen and not be bothered by some idiot fumbling beside me. I mean if I want to do that the last place I'd do it is in the cinema. I like my full attention on the task in hand if you know what I mean.

No these days I have bigger concerns when I go to the cinema, I like to go to horrors because, if I can, I like to re-enact what I've seen. I'm the ultimate copycat killer. Lazy in murder as I am in everything. Screams and gasps are easily hidden with the inane crowd that flocks to these. I'm merely giving the survivors something they can remember forever.

I usually go for people on their own, the loners that not many will miss, I had one who wasn't discovered for three days. Three days! I haven't been to that cinema since. I mean, for fuck sake, clean the place. Today may be different as I can't think of a more deserving couple to serve my needs than the ones in front. If they're not glaring at me to stop laughing, but laugh I must, there gazing into each other's eyes instead of the screen. Sickeningly, simpering twats, turn my stomach more than the movie ever could.

Oh cool, only about twenty minutes left and it looks like the couple's going to get it. Yeah, while they are kissing straight through her head with the knife, he turns around and looks in horror as does his counterpart sitting in front of me.

I decide to do a little twist because he really is an obnoxious prick, on-screen he's stabbed in the heart while he leans over to try and restrain the attacker. I go straight for the throat, great neither have the chance to scream, they collapse into each other, to the casual observer in the darkness they'll look like they're getting it on. I've no need to wait until the end I've had my happy ending, satisfaction and release coursing through my veins, heaven. I can't resist taking a quick photo, a selfie with them behind me, these phones are great, I can upload and mess around with it to my heart's content when I get home.

I love the movies, I always end up the star of the show, always the villain never the hero.

I buy more popcorn and coke I have work to do when I get home. My screen may be smaller but the viewing more enjoyable.

Mine

I was hooked on his dance moves first he always made me get into his groove and start to move. I then moved onto his eyes and was completely smitten. The only trouble was he was my best friend's new beau and beautiful he was. Right there and then I decided he was going to be mine and the beginnings of my demise began.

I could not stand seeing the two of them together but to get to him I had to keep Sandra around. That was hard to do when she had the same problem as me we were both obsessed with Tim.

I found out his schedule from Sandra's whispered phone calls. Learnt when he was dancing, playing football, bowling or table tennis. He was a fitness fanatic, I suppose along with his mother that's what made that fantastic body. The body I was soon going to be licking all over. I digress. I have to keep a steady head. I need to bide my time.

I suddenly took a keen interest in certain activities, Sandra was bemused. I told her I just did not want to pile on the pounds like her. My beloved friend I watched slowly move away from me bit by bit. I didn't care she was only still here at all, so I could keep tabs on Tim.

I started sneaking photographs of her and Tim just one now and again, she had an endless supply. I was making a space to keep a record of me and Tim and all our firsts. The first time we kissed and so on. I did have to cut Sandra out and paste me in but I completely forgot that fact when the finished product was under my pillow.

Poor Sandra stopped taking photographs every few weeks as she kept breaking out in some nasty rash and had swollen eyes and lips. Her allergy returned on and off but she never figured out what was causing it.

I could, I was injecting the very substance she was allergic to into her cream and watched with a smile as she slathered it all over her precious to Tim's face.

Stupid bitch kept asking my advice.

"Kelly, look at the state of me, what am I going to do?"

I told her she may be allergic to something in the pill and she better stop taking it for a while until she got her doctor to check it out. I then had to listen to her go on and on about how she'd have to curtail her sexual activities with Tim, I already knew that.

Today I am getting a makeover it's been three weeks and Kelly hasn't heard anything back from the doctor, she would never risk pregnancy. I'm hoping a virile young man will be just ripe for picking. He has no idea just how close me and Sandra once were as he never sees us together now. So that will be one moral dilemma solved for him.

Sandra was not the stupid bitch I thought she was. The resounding slap she landed on me when I was supposed to meet Tim I deserved. The tablets are now the beginning of my end.

Bye.

Expectations

On the outskirts of society always looking in, romance is an entity you heard described but never experienced for yourself forever left on the shelf.

Family life, never was, your dad hardly around, just because. Mama taught you that you avoided a slap if you kept her gin and tonic on tap. You were the man of the house, your sister teased with an open blouse.

You chased normality at every turn but your attempts at relationships crashed and burned. Friends thought you too in their face, your fervour they can't embrace.

Stalking is how you get your fix, always watching never having to mix. Families became your prey of choice, peaking through windows your vice. If mama was good you never met, but if she was bad, her routine you'd vet. The punishment you'd dish out, you loved to hear them shout.

If mama was playing offside, behind your balaclava you'd hide. Mama was in for some pain, sexual fulfilment your gain, orgasms you didn't feign.

Then you met the one, the mama you were unable to shun. Perfect in every way, loving to her kids, every day. She became your sole desire, the only one to light your fire. For the first time in your life, you felt love, called her your turtle dove.

The night he hit her you felt the blow, you knew it was time, he had to go. He was now the one you hunted, evidence gathering, senses blunted. With his mistress you indulged, with your hatred for him, you plunged.

He came to her defence as you knew he would, bludgeoned to death, you felt so damn good.

At his funeral, you glared with all your might, hoping she'd sense you, turn to you in her plight. You never have seen such sadness, her, the kids, to grieve for him, madness.

You have met her now a few times volunteering at the kid's school they all love your rhymes. She smiles at you but it never reaches her eyes, the hurt he caused her you are quick to despise.

It's the older one's birthday and you have been invited, to actually be in the house, you're beyond excited. She's thanking you for coming and shakes your hand, your having a moment where you stand.

She asks you to cut the cake, you're doing your best not to shake.

All your dreams are coming true the future is now down to you.

You see nights gazing into each other's eyes, hers hypnotise. Happiness personified through days you glide.

This is going to be your family, picture-perfect it will be.

Fresh Meat

Ah, a brand new slab of fresh meat. It took a lot of time and energy getting it here and deserves my full attention to make it perfect, or at least tastier than last time. I've acquired a hook to hang the meat don't know exactly what this is for, I've heard the term curing. It reminds me of healing but there ain't no doctor that can heal this creature. As I hang it a pool of blood begins to form and congeal at my feet, messy business this. I whistle for Rover who needs no instruction and immediately starts salivating and lapping, one job is taken care of.

Blast, the bloody doorbell I throw on a pair of overalls and lock the door of the shed. My catch and Rover safely hidden away from prying eyes. Using my peep-hole I see it is my mother, interfering bitch always seems to know when I'm enjoying myself. She must have her peep-hole into my brain I wouldn't want to see into hers there would be nothing to hold my interest. I supply the expected tea and biscuit and the small talk.

After my usual non-committing shrugs, resistance is futile, I have yet another date I grudgingly admire her persistence. She leaves happy in the knowledge that this one could be the one, maybe one day she'll pick the right sex.

A quick wash and back to the shed Rover licking his lips. I shoo him outside and close the door. I need privacy for this bit. I'm a lot more prepared than last time. I run my hand over the meat a bit bristly in places I grab my razor and carefully shave, ah yes lovely and smooth. Next, I grab the oil and rub it all over, I can't wait any longer remove my overalls and add my special juice to the mix, it's the only relief I get these days.

I am now disgusted with myself and the meat, it must be disposed of. I dress and let Rover back in he will do some of the work for me. Now for the rest of the prep, a nice bottle of red I think. I boiled the meat last time a wee bit salty and dry for my taste, I went for younger prey this time hopefully it will be extra tender. Rover doesn't go for stir-fry so I think some steak will go down well. I did a big shop last week as I am expecting not to need meat for a while. I told the nosy girl at the till that my new girlfriend was vegetarian and I was giving it a go. Onions chopped, spuds peeled, time to go get the meat.

Rovers busy chewing a finger he likes the bony bits. I have acquired a cleaver it does a much cleaner job, speaking of jobs maybe I'll become a butcher. I'm getting hands-on experience. Turning the meat in the pan, Rover waiting expectantly at my feet, I think we'll have it rare.

Palatable

Oh how I love The Black House, fun and debauchery abound. Every Friday I come and my dastardly actions always go unheeded until I'm well gone. I have my own little nook where I secrete myself with a book until some interesting or exotic bird of the female persuasion catches my eye. I never actually read the book but I find if you frequent any bar book in hand you are left in relative peace except for a few snorts of derision now and again.

I'm going to stockpile a few whiskies, so I can survey my prey without showing my hand too early. The barman is used to my appearance so doesn't flinch at my pale skin any more. He doesn't even attempt the petty small talk just takes my money and nods. We have a little arrangement where if I see something I like I let him know and he, in turn, lets me know what the object of my desire's chosen tipple is. I often wonder if he knows but he never lets on.

If I just wanted sex it would be so much easier, as that's what a lot of people come here for, but I have a taste for blood, pumping, flowing, blood. The exhibitionist in me needs the little scare that this may be it I just might be caught, ah the extra thrill of fellow drinkers breezing by as I indulge my taste-buds. I have been known to get too excited and have to retire to my little nook to remove the skin from my fangs and replace their covering veneers. No, before you ask I am not a vampire, I paid a fortune in dentistry to get my fangs, just so. I won't die if I don't get my fill just fester in boredom and misery.

Ah, now she looks interesting, nice and petite, I thought the big-boned girls would have a meatier taste at one time, but I was wrong, all that fat and extra flavours just get in the way of that glorious blood. I tend not to waste my time so catch the bar mans eye so he's aware of that she's drinking. Oh, how ironic it's a Bloody Mary, love it.

I gesture for him to pour me a double Bloody Mary and it's sent over. I pop in my little pill and am ready to go. It just makes them a little drowsy, I'm not doing any harm, but they never have the will or energy after partaking to stop my suckling. They'll explain away their cut in the morning thinking the sex got a wee bit energetic and will be too ashamed to mention to anyone a one-night stand.

She accepts my offering with elegance and we retire to my little nook. The lump she takes out of my neck is sure to leave a scar and those fangs are real. The barman acknowledges my terrified yelp and pops a little pill in my whisky apparently I suckled his niece on his night off. Revenge is always on the menu in The Black House.

Purged

Constantly battling my demons, they never leave me alone. Whispering day and night, you're no good, you should never have been born, why torment me this way? Voices that taunt, belittling, and egging me on. I cut my wrists to keep them at bay. The pain satisfies them for a while. The demons play with me, toy with me, paw at me. Their paranoid and controlling, they feed on my fear. They've called me whore, slut and bitch. Mummy silences them now and again with a hug and a kiss.

They like to dress me up pretty and buy me little gifts. I parade in front of the mirror and at my reflection, I hiss. I'm their property they own all of me, say without them where would I be? Cover me with their special scent, Eau de skunk, pissing all over my lamppost, there often blinding drunk.

They like to feed, they like me fat, I am making my own welcome mat, the weight hides many a hurt. They breathe in every pore I can not wash them off. They follow me to school and control my pen. They scribble all over my art I have to do it again. Their vile thoughts control my speech they swear at all my friends. They sit on my shoulder and rain on my parade. They like me on my own, vulnerable and scared.

I'm never free, they reside in my head often I wish I was dead. I've pulled out my hair at its roots, fidgeted and yanked, anything to try and stop their assault. I've prised off my fingernails thinking part of them is living there, I can feel them crawling. I've wet myself in fright they've cackled and heckled in delight, revelling in my plight.

Sometimes they're my friend and I think it's all come to an end, they make me smile for a while. When counsellors visit they smile and are serene when she's not looking there tweaking in my brain, driving me insane.

No-one will believe me, I'm sick you see. They've poked until I've bled and said if I tell I'm dead.

Tonight I've had enough the demons are going to pay.

I slice from ear to ear, now at them, I jeer "Put your dick away, daddy, no playtime today."

Learnt

Soft as butter they said, does not have a bad bone in her body they said. A loving home, warm bed and plenty of food would help anyone's disposition. Walks and games were plentiful I loved my family and they loved me.

It was a sad day when George left us, a heart attack. My walks and playtime became fewer and farther in between. There was days of no food but tears and calling for George did she not know he was gone? I took matters in hand woke here with gentle licks on days she didn't want to get up. Learnt to bring my bowl to her not just for me it reminded her of food and we often ate together. My lead, which I shook at her, was ignored but I am nothing if not a persistent bugger.

Ten minutes stretched to twenty and some days she got the lead herself. A person called Tony became a regular attendee at our walks all over us like a rash. He made her laugh so I accepted him.

I brought her the lead one day an engaging smile on my face.

"Sorry Milly not today. Tony's coming for dinner need to clean the house and me up."

Dejectedly, tail between my legs I retreated to my bed. She hummed and danced around the house. She dusted and kissed Georges picture and asked him if it was okay, he again never answered.

Tony came with a ball for which I had no interest. He gave me a sneaky kick when Lucy was out of the room. I stayed out of his way as much as I could after that. He stayed the night no call upstairs for cuddles with Lucy.

He moved in and made my life miserable.

Bit by bit pieces of George started disappearing I retrieved his photo from the bin. I was no longer allowed inside so George shared my kennel with me.

On occasions that Lucy was out, he would bring me in and torment me. Cigarette burns to my underbelly became the norm. I became very depressed, stopped eating. Lucy eventually took me to the vet who queried my cuts and burns. I was not allowed home as an investigation had to take place. Tony was fined, Lucy broke it off, and I was allowed home.

Blissful weeks followed. Lucy and I revelled in each other's company.

One night I heard a voice I recognized and snuggled up closer to Lucy trembling with fear. He barged in, grabbed me, and threw me with brutal force across the room. I yelped in pain, Lucy screamed at him to leave me alone, and that she was calling the police. He slapped her hard but it was when I saw the lit cigarette that I lost it. He was not doing that to Lucy. I took a running jump and latched onto his throat. I only stopped shaking my prey when he stopped squealing. I learnt how to get food by myself.

Community Service

It's Halloween and they're out looking for treats. He gets chatting to his mates and forgets about his little sister. At the next house, he asks her in, she calls out for her brother but he doesn't hear her, or maybe he does but she's annoying to him at best of times, so he shrugs it off.

She walks in at the promise of candy. He drugs her and treats himself to a large brandy. He watches her, snoring deeply, conked out on his settee and rubs his hands with glee.

He sits, still watching her, each snore sounds like a purr. He'll tie her up soon because he wants her awake when her innocence he takes.

Licking his lips, he caresses her hips. She's dead to the world and he must stay controlled. It won't be half as much fun if he does it now, not enough damage would be done.

He wants her awake and screaming, for years he's been dreaming of a moment like this. She's a redhead, her veins easily read, as if she's been kissed by fire. Everything about her fuelled his desire. He goes to the window, the brother and his friends seem to have gone, I wonder if he's missed her yet, chasing his own girl, I bet.

His chemicals are ready all will be gone even her teddy. One day he'll be caught but it's years since he's been on anyone's radar. He's the local clean-up guy, the one who everyone thinks is shy. He's always ready to please, forever plastering knees.

Always vigilant constantly observing to his own needs serving. He'll help look for her in every cranny and nook, offering tea and sympathy, trusted by the community.

Please just Say

I saw something the other day, I wish I hadn't because with me it has not easily lain. I was at the swimming pool collecting my neighbour's little boy when this girl caught my eye.

There was nothing particularly noticeable about her except she seemed to be lost she had this look of sadness that was drowning her from the inside out. She caught me turned away from my stare she threw me an angry glare.

None of this is what upset me I wouldn't like a stranger staring at me either. It was the bruises I saw when she turned around, the area they were in that hurt me most profound.

I knew in my heart that girl was being abused, misused. Why it hasn't easily laid I turned away, nothing to nobody did I say, I rue the day.

Not Over

You wrecked the good chunk of our marriage, the love that floated the horse and carriage. It began the first time you laid an angry finger. I couldn't forgive, couldn't get it out of my head, forever it lingered.

It coloured everything I did and said, I thought of ways to make you dead. The idea of killing you was so tempting, the planning and dreaming kept me sane, picturing your demise helped me deal with the pain. Every time you hit me I had an epiphany a knife, tablets, shotgun, I imagined each one

I looked up assassins online while drinking copious amounts of wine. I don't even like wine but it felt disrespectful to make it enjoyable research, I can celebrate after.

It was not a cheap option and I saved religiously. Each time you sneered or jeered I added to the pot. I became submissive, no arguments at ours. You revelled in my obedience but still now and again you managed to convince yourself that I needed a hit.

I am now addicted to painkillers and I'm a raving alcoholic. I have spent all the money on keeping myself topped up and sane. You hang both addictions over me. Your idea of love was always wrapped up in an iron glove.

Last night was the last straw when you beat me raw. The tablets I squash give me a satisfying hug as I add them to your drink and food.

You never woke up, I smiled when accidental death was recorded. It was meant to finish us, make it all over, but every day I visit your grave, kneel and pray. Cleaning and polishing your headstone, still your willing slave.

She's your Last

She's a beauty but twisted just a little bit, luring with the flash of a tit. She's a wee bit off-kilter, her Daddy's good little girl, her communion gift a necklace of pearl.

On her birthday he gave her a paper crown, for a moment she feels like a queen daddy's real present can never be seen.

He died on a Sunday she remembers it well, Mammy grieved and she still couldn't tell. She didn't want to ruin her memory of him as he had fulfilled her every whim. She didn't know the monster I knew even when my belly grew. I killed his bastard with a coat hanger nearly ended me as well. It was the same one I used to cut his throat it gave me such pleasure to kill the randy old goat. The burglary tale went down well if they ever doubted I couldn't tell.

Each new lover takes on his face, even when they are good to her she turns their actions into a disgrace. She washes them clean burns the wig and party dress. The police still seeking a murderess, they are aware are of her intelligence and good looks.

She has no shortage of game each time she uses a new name. The setting will be wonderful, you'll enjoy the dance, shes your last romance.

When?

Waiting for the Luas in Tallaght, minding my own business when this little bugger stops and spits on my shoe, laughs and runs off. No reason, no explanation, no apology, nothing. I'm more disgusted with myself because I hang my head in shame and say what I feel I am, nothing. What have I got to be ashamed about, but I am. I'm ashamed of my apathy, my fear. I meet the eyes of the fella on my left and he says "Bastard, no respect". I nod and say "thanks". What am I thanking him for? For his observing that the bugger showed no respect or is he making comment on me because he's right, I have no respect for myself. I'm the invisible middle-aged woman who got noticed because someone spits on my shoe.

Why can't they notice that if they smile, I smile back, that I can hold a conversation and even on occasions be witty? I never was much of a looker but think I have got an ok personality. When did that fade into the background? When did I disappear? At what time of my life did this happen?

Ah here comes the tram, pre-paid ticket so no chat to the driver. I daren't talk to another passenger, be intruding on their space. Well, that's what I think. So is the problem with me, am I giving off some vibe, or is society sinking daily into everyone for themselves mode. Don't need or want to interact with anyone unless there's something in it for me.

I still haven't wiped the spittle from my shoe. It reminds me that there has to be a change, a change, in me. That I'm worth more. I smile to myself, the teenager in the row across avoids my gaze and squashes himself into the window if he could crawl through it he would. He obviously thinks I've lost it, this makes me giggle. Or maybe he saw me go back and kill that little fucker.

Is it any wonder I travel alone? It makes sorting little shits out so much easier. I amuse myself all the way home thinking of the pee that ran down the little runt's trousers, sometimes the best company is your own, but only sometimes, worth remembering that.

Bored

Just going to write and see what pops into my head extremely bored at work. Stagnating in the Public service - ha public who are they I never see them. I'm paid to sit quietly while my brain rots till nothingness creeps into my soul, and when there having just as equally a boring day or they need to break the mood for a while they call me Clerical Officer 50167, come here and shut the door.

Then I get the lecture on my supposed inadequacies re. doing a job I haven't been given. I'm too apathetic to care I sit there nod, agree, apologise, it pays my bills this crap existence.

Right now I probably look the busiest I've done all day sitting here typing away. My boss has walked by me twice and actually smiled at me. He thinks I'm being useful, I am, I'm releasing the poison from my veins onto this page. This page should be burning, along with all my files taking over my desk space. I better move them a bit tomorrow, put some away in a draw I'll take them out again next week.

So people go study get the Leaving Certificate, decide to go for a cushy public service job, no bonuses, no company car and slowly productively fade to nothingness.

Maybe I'll be one of those people they find dead at my desk my body hiding behind my pretend to file well I can dream, can't I? I don't know what they'll think of my collection, all the body of old colleagues over the years. I'm sure like me they'll be forgotten soon enough. Gaining notoriety is known to be tough.

Mute

I couldn't kill her because she's not a man but I had to stop her though she's my biggest fan. I can never let her tell or follow my wicked ways. I don't need any competition and I don't want to become the latest craze.

I cut out her tongue so with it I can never be betrayed on my mantle it's hung, beautifully portrayed. She's tied up in a cage in the corner and gazes at her tongue mournfully.

Now she will never tell or scream. It's great living with someone who never argues, just nods, smiling maniacally. Her fingers are framed and placed artistically on my sitting room wall, see she had started to sign, and I couldn't leave her with any ways of communicating, could I.

Haunted

In the corner huddled, naked. I'm more colourful than any clothes I could wear. I'm red, black, and blue. Battered and bruised, my crime enquiring about his whereabouts. Together for 6 years now, our beautiful son asleep upstairs and I'm not entitled, according to him, to ask him anything.

I'm replaying my actions and conversation over and over again. He's never raised his hand to me before. I realise this didn't just spring up out of nowhere. For weeks now it's been building money worries, new baby, never having lived together before. He can't handle it, he can't even handle the thought of being a dad, he acts as if he hates him. I believe he's jealous of him.

Maybe it's just a one-off, I wipe my nose and my hands covered in snot, tears and blood. I have to get up, I have got a baby to look after, he can't see me like this. I need to shower, I can wash away the blood but not the shock and fear. He hasn't gone near me since the birth and last night with the first punch his erection appeared. It grew the more he hit me. The names he called me, the force he used. I can't tell my parents, they didn't want me to move in with him in the first place. "I'm nineteen" I had told them "an adult and a new mum with a fellah that adores me I'll be fine." How can I now go back and tell them they were right?

It's four months on and middle of summer and I'm clad in a woolly over-sized sweater which hides a multitude. He's got clever and hits me in places which can be hidden from everyone, but he doesn't hide his beatings from his son. In fact, I think he waits until he's asleep in my lap sometimes to start. He knows I'm more afraid of him hurting him than me.

Yesterday something in me snapped I'm not taking any more. My son's not taking it anymore. We both deserve better.

In walks the oppressor, I usually sit waiting to suss out his mood before I do anything but not today. I carry on reading a book, Paul's asleep in his cot oblivious. He glares at me walks into the kitchen, and comes storming back.

"Where's my tea, you know what time I get in at and my tea and dinner should be already prepared sitting on the table waiting for me."

"Paul and I have already eaten and since the last time I prepared food it ended up all over me and the kitchen I've decided I won't be doing that anymore." His face is incredulous in any other situation it would be hilarious actually, even now it's hilarious. I start to giggle and can't stop, nothing could have stopped it. "Have you finally lost the plot, stupid bitch, what's funny?"

I stand up and ask him for once can we take our fight into a different room and let the baby sleep in peace. I start walking before he gets a chance to respond, he comes in arm raised and stops mid-air as he catches sight of the carving knife in my hand. I slice and only succeed in ripping his shirt. He starts apologizing the only time since the first time, tells me he loves me, he'll never hit me again. I can feel my resolve breaking and need to get to my son. I start walking and he grabs me the knife clatters to the floor. I knew there and then I was going to pay for this, big time.

He goes in and wakes up Paul puts the disturbed toddler in his walking chair and hands him the knife. I beg him to take it off him but he walks over to me and spits in my face. I tell him I'll do anything he wants, that I love him but just take the knife off the baby. He pushes me on my knees and makes me go on all fours and rapes me while my son gurgles and plays with the knife. Not a scream or whimper do I make but hum and make soothing noises so Paul won't get alarmed. When he's finished he gets up and urinates on me and Paul.

I've never known such hate and haven't experienced it on the same level since.

When he leaves the next day I pack up all his stuff and our stuff I ring my parents and beg them to get me out of there, and plead with them can I come home. I hear my mother sobbing in the background and my dad says "Darling, we've been dying for this call. It killed us the last time when you asked us to leave and not come back. We'll be there right away." I never told them about the rapes, too ashamed, but the latest beatings were obvious you only had to look at me.

The drive home is terrifying and soothing at the same time. I knew I'd done too much growing up I could never go back to the girl that lived with mammy and daddy again, I wasn't the same girl.

He killed himself in a prison cell, I didn't send him there, it was an awful crime committed on someone else. It was a twisted relief knowing Paul would never have to see him and a twisted sadness because he'd been my first love and for a long time I adored him.

Time and life move on.

Scars heal, hope returns but your past is always your past and a part of me will be haunted forever.

Possessed

They never asked why I set the tree on fire just dragged me kicking and screaming blood streaming from my nose. They didn't let me stay to watch if it burn to the ground.

That tree has been my nightmare for years but lately, it's haunted my days as well. Its bite way worse than its bark, sharp tendrils pinching me like the teeth of a baby shark.

At first, my child's brain thought it was fairies I'd seen playing at the tree, I thought it was their meeting place. I realized eventually they weren't playing when I saw the witch step from the tree and swallow their cuteness one by one.

I put it down many times to just a bad dream and for a long time barricaded it from my view until the night when there was a tip-tapping at my window and when I removed the pillows there was the tree manically grinning at me. My parents hushed me to sleep told me it was just my imagination but I knew better. I removed the barricades I needed to keep a close eye on my enemy.

I took up karate but the tutor got annoyed because I just wanted to learn how to attack as if a ninja possessed. I had no interest in self-defence because in my mind I already knew if I was ever to have a chance against the witch I would have to take her completely by surprise.

I begged my parents to chop her down but they said no because she blossomed so prettily in the summer, I gawped, my fear was no substitute for her beauty apparently. I later heard them whispering that they couldn't give in to me it was something I would grow out of.

She whistled at me whenever it was windy and tried to lull me into a false sense of security on beautiful sunny days but I would not be fooled, she was a wolf in sheep's clothing.

I secreted the matches for a long time I had to have enough to do the job and waited for the time that they would both leave me alone. That was today when I ran at the tree full force assuming I would knock her out and broke my nose. Slobbering and sniffing blood and spit I lit the sticks I had secreted and placed at the base of the tree. I finally got a flame and watched with glee, I thought I heard a scream.

I heard it was my mother rushing out to save me. I sit and watch Dr Kavanagh as she keeps trying to cajole information out of me but she never gets anywhere and never answers my question either. "Did I burn it to the ground?" My parents don't answer it either but I can sit in this clinic until they let me go home and see for myself. I worry about them constantly.

Voyeur

The usual scenario he asks me to dance and that's it talking is over. He can't take his eyes off me but I think I'm the one more focused, the watched, watching the watcher. He has an outfit laid out before I arrive, his studio all set up. I work hard trying to come up with new routines and steps and I never know what music I'll be dancing to. Ah, he's looking for contemporary today, well that's how I interpret this one, and it always causes a smug smile on his face – Private Dancer.

I swirl, I pirouette, I jump and no I'm distracted, and stumble, he's gazing out the window. My swan song is nearing I thought I felt his eyes wandering lately, his stare not so intense. I can't handle not seeing him every week and I've reached my limitations I can't get better than I am right now. He rushed over and asks am I okay. His concern pushed me over the edge I excuse myself and lock the bathroom door. I also can be prepared. I open the cabinet, remove the tablets and plastic glass. I take them relishing the dryness of each one.

Returning, my moves sluggish and uncoordinated, he escorts me to a chair. He sits on the floor looking up at me and I collapse into his arms. It was our last date and our last dance. He pays her family the fee, and the voyeur moves on to his next prodigy.

Little Boy

I saw this angelic little boy, eyes blue, big head of blond curls which he'll bemoan in years to come, gorgeous smile. I realise he's alone, can't be more than three. I get down on my hunkers and spread my arms he doesn't hesitate. Oh, the innocence as he clasps me in a wondrous hug. I try to get him to talk but he keeps squeezing my nose and breaking into laughter, he's adorable. Putting him down I take his hand. I noticed things now that I hadn't, his hands grubby, skin peeling and sore, curls all knotted, not a nice smell.

I walk him around see can I find who he belongs to. This woman comes running, screaming, grabs him, and slaps him. He doesn't cry, gives a resigned shrug. What I thought was innocence was joy, in someone willing to give him some attention.

This was a boy who didn't cry, mature beyond his years, he's learnt no point in tears, they won't feed or comfort. The woman rounds on me, anger spurting from her core, screams at the top of her lungs "Have you no children of your own, leave mine alone?"

She looks high I would have avoided her like the plague if it wasn't for the lad. I wish I could take him but what gives me the right. I watch my eyes welling up as he says "sorry, mommy" takes her hand and leads her home. I might take that little boy him next time he roams.

I'll never get the opportunity as I open the paper the next day and he is headline news. He and his mother are found dead in their apartment. It is not known yet whether it was the mother or someone else. I'll never forgive myself, the horror of living with the fact that if I reported her I may have been able to save him.

The Wall

I'm sorry we are having a fight it is just that when things bother me I go quiet. I've always been the same I build things up inside, they may be small but because there held in so long they sit and turn my insides into a festering pit.

The smallest slight can then become a raging tornado, an uncontrollable reaction that doesn't fit the supposed crime and even though I know all this, I can't stop, at the moment I'm still mad a major disagreement because of all the little tiffs we never had.

I think this kettle has had a good brewing in my intestinal wall, it's been stewing and now it's come to the boil. I'll have to handle things better and talk about the niggling stuff or I'll never handle a real patch of rough.

I'm writing instead of talking to you digging my heels in, not answering your call refusing to scale this wall. This wall that I've built, maybe if I give it a little tilt, an inch more, no I can't scale it yet. It's looming too large on my horizon I'm not ready to tear it down yet.

I'm sorry hun I'm trying but it's taken years to build this wall and now its oh so tall. Maybe it will mature and stoop, fade into the background and stop tying me in a loop. It will be on a later date, one that I hope is not too late.

But not today I'm sorry are the words I keep saying after you wanted to make up and surprised me by sneaking in. I'm sorry, I repeat over and over again, as I remove the knife.

Justice

He was always ready with hugs and affection too much so on reflection. Forever lavishing her with sweets and toys frowning when she played with boys.

I was so delighted he took the time they were bonding with songs and rhyme. He had her forever sitting on his knee. Why didn't I see? See that something wasn't right, he didn't even notice me when she was around, I wasn't on his radar.

Then there was that dreadful day I'll never forget, she came to me and said: "Sorry mommy, I'm wet, I didn't mean it."

I was about to reprimand as it been years since there were any toilet accidents but as I examined her I saw that her panties were covered in blood. I knew then that he been up to no good.

I tried to stay calm and not frighten my little lamb.

"What happened darling, tell mommy everything."

She started crying and said, "you will say I'm lying."

"He told me to say I fell Mommy, I'm not allowed to tell he said you would die if I told anyone."

My heart sank to the floor my innocent girl, no more.

"I'm not going anywhere, dear and I'm certainly not dying. We'll go and see Doctor 'G' he'll make it better, you'll see."

He took over from there all I could do was vacantly stare.

How could I not have known?

I asked myself over and over again as I rang his phone. I told him where I was, and that she was bleeding. He denies all wrongdoing "She must have fallen, always bloody running," he said.

The court case is looming on the horizon, about five years the police are surmising. I've already bought the gun, take lessons on Tuesdays at one.

Only five years is a disgrace, it will have to be me that will wipe the smile off his face.

Reaction

I can't believe I'm getting married. I was engaged before at seventeen to my first love who I met at thirteen. I thought he was gorgeous that he could do no wrong.

Six years on I'm red, black, and blue. Battered and bruised, my crime inquiring about his whereabouts. Our beautiful son upstairs and I am not entitled, according to him, to ask. For weeks this has been building, money worries, new baby, living together. He can't handle being a dad, he hates him. He's jealous.

I wipe my nose and my hands covered in snot, tears and blood. I need to shower I can wash away the blood but not the shock and fear. No sex since the birth and last night with each punch his erection appeared. It is summer and I'm in a woolly over-sized sweater which hides a multitude.

He's back and I ask him can we take our fight elsewhere? I leave before he responds he comes in arm raised and stops mid-air when he sees the carving knife. I slice and only succeed in ripping his shirt. He apologizes, the only time since the first time, tells me he loves me, he'll never hit me again. I feel my resolve breaking and need to get to Paul. He grabs me, the knife clatters to the floor. I knew I was going to pay, big time.

He wakes up Paul, puts him in his walker with the knife. I beg him to take it off him but he laughs. I say I'll do anything he wants, that I love him. He pushes me on my knees makes me go on all fours and rapes me while Paul gurgles and plays with the knife. Not a scream or whimper do I make but hum and make soothing noises so Paul won't get alarmed. I've never known such hate and haven't experienced it since.

I was nineteen when that relationship ended and for years it shaped my life.

I didn't go near men for at least five years, concentrating on being a good mum. I heard he killed himself in a prison cell, I didn't send him there, it was an awful crime committed by him on someone else. It was a twisted relief knowing Paul would never have to see him and a twisted sadness because he'd been my first love and for a long time I adored him.

I met George in the supermarket of all things and fell for him hard, a little row, no such thing for me, became a huge deal. I decided I couldn't go through it all again, and prepared him a last supper. The poison I kept in the shed and hadn't used in a while became useful again. I cried when he died.

Broken

Darkness envelops me in its warmth, the shadows calling me I drown in its embrace. I avoid mirrors these days because my reflection jeers, bitterness etched on my face. A long black curl in my sheets grabs my attention, one of my conquests too many to mention. It would of being a woman back in the day, and I'd smile and probably in her scent, lay. These days it's from the dog still sleeping like a log. I smile sardonically, woe is me, what used to stand up and open the door now stares mournfully at the floor. I pick up the curl and let it carry back to yesteryear, to a face I still hold dear.

She was my fountain of youth, stopped me from being a brute. She kept all my demons at bay from her I never let my mind stray. Now that she's gone I chase my darker days, drug-induced, I'm constantly in a haze. No longer areas of grey just black or white and I hide from the light.

The long back curl has caused my emotions to unfurl. She would have hated seeing me like this, would have said I was taking the piss. Today at some stage I'll cut, just so for that moment, this memory I can shut. I'm too much of a coward to end it all but revel in watching the blood fall. See, she died running away from me, trying to remove her vision of me, me, wrapped around our friend, both nearing the end.

Her face I'll never forget, it makes my pillows wet. I'm torturing myself daily, memories haunt gaily. The car flung her into the air blood matted her long black hair. She was an angel, a sweet soul she'd hate me drowning in this hole. I hope she has forgiven me but I'll never know so I live in misery.

Around my head emotions twirl, brought on by one long black curl, I am forever bound, searching for relief that's not to be found.

My Home

Self-appointed janitor surveys his domain. His Armour is his belief that he is not insane. His payment is his satisfaction that this place still stands he keeps it clean with his own bare hands.

The bodies of trespassers are dispersed throughout, creatures of all shapes and sizes are given some clout. Nothing is wasted, it can be used as decoration it's tonight's meal, devoured with zeal. His clothes are the covering from many of these the shells from a tortoise protect his knees.

He's heard rumbles and whispers from his hiding place, that his home is an eyesore, a disgrace. Talk of a shopping mall bandied around, he planted traps in the grounds. Chiselling bones with gusto great weapons can be made, you know. His only companion he calls rover, he tries training him to attack over and over. Rover thinks it's a great game and with licks responds to his name.

Besides his home, Rover is his love, no roof so he constantly converses with the man above.

Replaying in his mind his all-consuming mantra, "This is my coliseum, my castle beware of causing me any hassle."

Too high a Price

Marriage is my prison wall, my husband my warder. The kitchen sink is my daily chore, no window that would be too interesting for me. I remember a joke my uncle was fond of saying "Dad why do brides wear white?" "Son, all kitchen appliances come in white." Many a true word said in jest, I should have heeded those words.

I listen to his breathing, out sunning himself in the garden, today I was allowed to open the patio doors, probably so he can hear me if I stop working for a minute. Our kids, the reason I stay, whenever they ask him anything he says ask 'her' indoors and he goes back to his snores. I have been demoted to 'her' I do not even have a name anymore.

I was a reluctant bride may as well have been a gun at my side. Pregnancy, my parents insisted. Wealthy and embarrassed I was constantly harassed. They could not take the shame so put money in my name, but I had to stay married for a period of ten years, but it would secure me and my baby for life. I did not hate him then; thought eventually I would fall in love. The twins are now five my soul is striving to survive; they never did say what would happen in the case of his death. I think it's a bet I'm willing to take. I think this marriage may be his demise.

Addictive

Dr Kavanagh stared at me with disbelief. The results of my endoscopy had come in. I knew what he'd found when he put that camera down my insides. I had been addicted to eating strange and wonderful objects for years.

It started at ten I was playing with a fifty pence coin, which I accidentally swallowed. My usually unflappable mother did not know what to do when she saw her son flailing unable to breathe.

That was a wonderful adventure, ambulance, check-ups I never had such undivided attention. When I am down, I can eat a key or earphones or whatever is near.

Here the temptations are many and I can only resist for so long.

"Put down the stethoscope."

I open my mouth he screams "Nooooo."

Fallen

He was built like a tower, tall and strong, his hands broad yet long. I'd say nearer to seven-foot than six. If you split him into an apartment block, the lift does not quite reach the top floor, his mind a closed door.

His dreams are in the basement his thoughts always low; he has many times reached the depths of depravity, no deeper could he go.

I have been assigned to be his mentor in this apartment called the jail, the walls he tries to derail. If his block had an address it would be a Mentally Deranged lane, he feels no pain.

He tries to smile but it does not beguile. It is shaped like a sneer its coldness jeers. I am meek in his presence but fascinated by his essence. It is unfortunate that although not everything fits well, his parts do not really gel, women fall under his spell. I find that he gives me palpitations and would lose my job for him no hesitation. I think that I can change him my common-sense dim.

We have had conjugal visits that no one has approved, the apartment block has moved. He brings me to heights never reached before security has been breached. I approve all his mail and hover over fine detail. He gets what I approve of not the women swearing undying love.

We plan what we will do when he is free, I am already breaking the bonds of matrimony. My divorce is looming the costs booming. I am mesmerised and leading the way to my soul's demise.

I have reported that I think he was temporarily insane and therefore now that he is well to keep him locked up there is no gain. Lauded for my credentials my lift would go to Suite Presidential.

His release date is set, the prospects make me wet. On a blessed day, I await anxiously, hidden from a colleague's view, cannot show myself, not yet. He walks through the gate and no emotions he demonstrates. I wait until he gets some distance from the prison and toot the horn with precision. Three beeps we had agreed, when we were planting the seed. His steps quicken as I beckon.

About two feet from the car he collapses, I could not tell how much time lapses. Blood spurts from his shirt he is mortally hurt. Standing there triumphant is a dad in his daughter's photos clad. He has avenged her by killing to go to jail he is willing. He salutes me with glee I fall to my knees in misery.

I now reside in hell no-one rings my bell. I owned up to everything reality stings. Sacked in disgrace I hide my face. He haunts my days and nights I write my plight. It has become a bestseller, its reviews stellar. It brings me no enjoyment and I write my torment.

Crossed

I wish and wished to see the man and the moon. Years spent dreamily gazing at the night sky. My wish came true and he was not at all what I expected.

He made the moon gruesome, shrouded it in evil. The man used to be good but he has gone to the other side, through clouds with a cleaver he glides.

His malevolent grin spreads across the sky, his fishing rod a weapon that makes stars cry.

He spits down a shower of acid, I wish for invisibility and frantically search for somewhere to hide.

I now wish to never see the man in the moon, any time would be too soon.

Together Forever

He's looking this way again. I purposely, resolutely, ignore him as always, well since the first time that is. Try and ignore him I mean, as he must know he gives me the creeps, and he is always in the corner of my eye. He declared, that first time, his undying love for me, in glorious poetic prose, loudly and astride a chair in the school canteen. He called it 'Catriona my reason for Living'. I can only imagine the colour I must have become. I'm sure I could have lit up the whole school. My friends doubled up and I could get no sense or assistance from them. I or my friends don't find him funny anymore. The coffee he is drooling into is doing a terrible job of blocking the smell emanating from his armpits. For flip sake has he no friends or family to tell him.

He has in one way or another pestered us all. Collages of him and I have ended up in our lockers. Wedding and baby shower invitations, all from me, Catriona O'Dwyer, and him, Marcus Ryan. Anyone of the male persuasion he has spotted, daring to even glance in my direction, has been warned of he is an expert at cock blocking. He makes me feel guilty when I'm the innocent party, as my words bruised a lot more than my fists ever could. Whispered insults, loud titters, anyone who didn't know what was happening would have thought my friends and I were the aggressors.

He has taken some days to just issuing a plaintive cry, now and then. His latest offering to me, poetically, was 'Catriona my reason for Dying'. He is getting creepier daily. We have reported him to the Headmaster, Counsellors, anyone we thought would help him or us but he hasn't stopped. All the detentions, talks, may have slowed him down, but that's all. The police were never called as apparently, he hadn't physically touched anyone so far it was just a case of a boy mooning over a girl. I at one time thought that he may have been special - as in deficient - and to be pitied.

He may indeed have some personality disorder which will take someone more qualified than I to discover. Academically he is in the top five of the whole school. I am an average student so it's not my brainpower he's after, I know that for definite.

All of a sudden he stands upright, so abruptly that his chair falls to the ground, disrupting anyone in the vicinity that may have been having a sneaky doze. Marcus does not do embarrassment so there's no scarlet blushing or muffled apologies. In two long strides, he appears in front of me and like a cat leaving a present, deposits a single rose. I don't acknowledge his presence anymore and lifting the rose as if it were a decapitated mouse left by the aforementioned cat, I deposit the rose in the nearest bin. I hear him take a sharp intake of breath, I don't know why it still affects him so, he should be well used to my reaction by now.

I leave the canteen head held high my friends trailing, giggling, behind me, although these days its more out of nervousness than badness, the giggling that is. He turned his hands into the shape of a gun and picked us off one by one. Once I've left, I'm told by others that he just sits back down and resumes eating as if nothing had happened. I have thought of leaving the school and starting again but then that would mean he'd won. It's not worth losing the great friends I've made because of one cretin. I will have to get on to the school's social committee again though and make sure they never lift his barring order. It's my only escape from him when at school, and I don't think I could stay if he started turning up at them.

Our prom is coming up and I had hoped someone would have asked me by now. Maybe he's put the word out that no-one should. I open my locker and streamers, papier Mache love hearts, and an abundance of glitter lips all pour out onto the floor.

I sit despairingly in the middle of them, one of my friends hands me an envelope, I knew before I opened it would be from him. It was an invite and a picture with Marcus and me's face superimposed on a couple emblazoned with banners and crowns declaring them the new king and queen. I tear it up and Lydia says "You should have kept that for evidence". I turn on her spitting my words out tinged with malice "I've told you they will do nothing, unless he physically harms me, how many times do you have to be told that". One look at her crestfallen face and I am instantly apologetic and open my arms wide. In two minutes it's forgotten about, but we have a mess to clean and a plan to forge. Something has to be done.

That night I toss and turn and in the morning the idea that had hijacked me the night before hasn't gone away. What if I ask him to the prom on the proviso that afterwards, he leaves me alone and never bothers me again. I look in the mirror and remonstrate with myself, that he's finally done it, I'm as mad as he is. It makes sense though he's getting what he's asked for the last three years, a date, and a chance. What could go wrong? All my friends and the rest of the school will be there. They'll probably insist on a chaperone or two, it's just about the safest place I could ever meet him. You never know, maybe, once the thrill of the chase is over, he may not want to know any more. We've never had a conversation, not a proper one, he may find me boring as hell, I certainly intend to give it a good go. I send a text to my friends asking them to meet me. I'm going to tell them about my plan.

"Are you insane? Seriously, have you been tested? There's no way any of us is going to stand idly around and let this travesty happen."

Lydia's outburst is greeted with silence, she is flabbergasted. "Can someone please agree with me here, we can't allow her to do this, for starters its social suicide, and secondly he's madder than she is."

John shushes Lydia, "Actually, Catriona may be onto something here. I'll help her with it if she agrees on a double date. How's about it Lydia? Me, you and the delightful couple Catriona and Marcus".

Lydia has gone every colour. She has always had a soft spot for John she won't turn this chance down. Everyone's attention is on her right now and I'm glad of the moments reprieve.

"Okay, I'll do it but only if you promise to never leave me, not even for a second, alone with creepy Marcus".

"I promise to never leave your side all evening, madam. I shall pick you and Catriona up, and then we'll all go and get Marcus safety in numbers and all that."

I decide to not hang about and that evening I pen an invite to Marcus asking him to the prom. Next day I give it to one of our dodgier friends and ask him to make sure it gets in Marcus's locker. The fact that he doesn't ask me anything about it, lets me know that the school's grapevine is working as well and as quickly as always. The crowd gathering in the vicinity of Marcus's locker is cruel and I tell them so. I ask them to please let me try and sort the whole thing out with at least embarrassment to me and him as possible. Sighs and murmurs abound, this is better than throwing a Christian into the lion's den for some of them. They are practically licking their lips in anticipation.

They just sneer and gather even closer. I hate my fellow humans sometimes. Marcus arrives earlier than usual I had been hoping I'd be well out of the vicinity by the time he got here. His face lights up when he sees me and if I could open a hole in the ground, I'd happily go into it. He takes my invite out and looks like he's going to come in his pants with excitement there and then. The jeers and hollers start, and he sinks to the ground and starts crying.

He looks at me with a look I've never seen before, disgust. He obviously thinks I planned all this, I run to his side, trying to explain, and he opens his rucksack and shoots me in the forehead. I die on the spot and levitate, somewhere, I don't know where, but watch as he kills everyone around him.

It ends when the police arrive and they shoot him on the spot, no attempt at talking him down. He flies over to me, takes my hand and says, "Hello, my love, now we're together, forever."

Enough

Oh lord, how has it come to this? Adoration turned to disgust. I can't stand the sight of him. His breathing annoys me in, out, snort, that bloody snort, makes me want to smash his face in. I had the iron in my hand one day and it would have been so easy. I stopped myself just in time. I don't even have a name any more. I'm the missus or her indoors to anyone around here. The kids call me mam and they were a great solace through the years. The teenage years have been and gone, and I have no desire to be here anymore. Why didn't I listen to my mother when she told me to keep a bank account, separate, just for myself? A ridiculous question I know why, I was stupidly, madly in love, I thought she was a harridan for even suggesting such a thing. The tinsel has long since fallen off my rose-tinted glasses.

He grunts and asks me, "Where did all the grocery money go?"

I tell him to turn sideways and look in the mirror. At another time, in the good old days, this would have caused laughter to us both, neither of us is laughing now.

"Oh, right smart ass aren't you? Think you are bleeding hilarious. Did you get me cigarettes?"

"I told you unless you give me extra I'm not including them in a shop anymore. There your own expense. I hate them, I'm one of those exes that harp on and on remember. Well, so you keep telling me anyway."

"You're a miserable old bitch, turn into your mother, that's not true your mother is a pussycat compared to you."

"You've sharpened my claws over the years, I had to fight back."

In three strides he's beside me and the punch he throws takes my breath away. He doesn't know that this time I came prepared. He's hit me many times over the years, but I swore to myself that the last one was absolutely the last one. As I rise the knife slides in easily, the look of shock and horror on his face makes me smile.

My flights are booked, and my case has packed, and I close the door on this hellhole for the last time, laughing maniacally as I hear him plead.

Pain

Pain is hidden under my sleeve, my bruises turning blue and green. He used to be so wonderful for the old him my heart grieves. He's gone nowhere to be seen, metamorphosed into a completely different being.

Now he hits me on a whim I don't have to do anything, I think my breathing annoys him, so I try to it as quietly as possible. I blame myself never think that it's just as the mood takes him so I try to his idea of perfection, in every way, to guess what he wants before he even knows what it is.

I can't believe he used to sing, woo me with his words, some songs he wrote just for me. I'm too scared to go, to run away tail between my legs, and even more afraid of staying.

I've lost friends long ago, he never wanted me to have any, and at the start, worshipped him, literally imagined he shitted gold. Not only did he poison them to me I also couldn't listen to more "leave him" begs.

I'm lying in a bed of my own making waiting for him to return in the silence, I can hear my heart breaking along with the bones and painful burn. The knife is sharpened I tested it on his cat, for once I can't wait for him to come home. He loved that cat as much as he hated me. He'll see her before he even gets to the bedroom door. I'll hear him before he sees me. He'll run to attack me like many times before, but this time it will be him that ends up prostrate on the floor.

Captured Image

What the hell? That's me?

I look gorgeous. This realization depresses me if it was a portrait of me now with all my flaws I would sue the ass of the artist. I scour the faces of my students. The more mature of them could actually look my image in the eye the others couldn't get past their redness or above their feet. Giggles and shuffling abound. As an art teacher I expect this reaction to life models, none of them recognize me. The teacher part of me is delighted don't need a whiff of scandal, the other my ego deflated.

I let my mind wander back, time travelling through my past a smile or grimace unwittingly traversing my face. The smile at the memory I have of falling and the grimace at how the love that I fell for was treating me.

The image on canvas is not how I felt I look thoroughly relaxed, oblivious to my surroundings and creator. In reality, every pore is screaming to run, I refuse to look up at him as I never liked the enforced posturing. It started as a bit of fun at first, two lovers exploring each other's boundaries and he declared me as his muse. You don't know how flattering that is until you are lauded as it. My inhibitions lessened with each stroke of his paintbrush and finger. Clothes getting smaller at each sitting until eventually none were needed. I revelled in his hungry eyes, relishing the effect I had on his paintbrush and elsewhere. We took many artistic breaks and indulged in other pleasures.

I thought I was his only one until I arrived home from a trip three days early undressing brazenly as I sauntered up the stairs. He could stroke me this evening but not with the brush although I was expecting a good licking, at least two coats. I heard them before I got to the door.

He was one of our best buyers always willing to pay over the odds and eager to see each new collection. I was going to withdraw and leave them to it when the scream of sexual pleasure emitted, let me know this was no ordinary business meeting. He had come to see Paul's etchings in the age-old cliched way. Barging in they were disentangling as I approached. They begged and cried for my forgiveness and the gun I bought so he would never leave me finally reached its destiny. The noise was so satisfying.

They became my muse I positioned them in different ways, had conversations and dressed them in different ways. I like to think one or two of my portraits captured some of their essences. I left when they began to rot.

I have spent many years trying to distance myself from Paul and those dark days. I used to redden with shame when I thought of our naughtier sittings getting into the wrong hands. Instead of a makeover I had a make under. Stopped wearing makeup, ditched the heels. Getting a degree was my new goal. I'm interrupted and taken from my nostalgic wandering by one of my students.

"Mrs Cassidy?"

"Nancy, my apologies, I think I got lost in the picture. I used to know her. Let's move on."

A merry Dance

First of all, let's get it right I'm not a dwarf or a gnome or as I've heard The Gingerbread Man. I'm a leprechaun/elf. How hard is that to grasp. My name is also Patrick, not Paddy or Grumpy, and most definitely not happy. I have never worn green as it clashes with my gloriously luxurious and long ginger beard. No the only colour I ever wear are various shades of red, so you may call it what you will with glorious gold buttons which sparkle and glitter in the sunlight. My hat is also red and yes it does usually have a belt buckle right in the centre. The fascination of human beings with my attire never fails to fascinate me. I do not slave all day over peoples thread worn and holey shoes, the treasure chest stories are true, I live off its proceeds very comfortably, thanks very much.

I adore solitude so when people come looking for the bag at the end of the rainbow I leave them on a merry uncomfortable journey there not likely to repeat. The Hamster Wheel debacle was my favourite as I created and masterminded that contraption with my mind and bare hands. That day if you had seen me you most likely would have been inclined to call me Happy. I nearly wet myself laughing watching grown men push each other, getting trapped and the wheel still rolling at times, killing one who thought he had escaped its grasp but getting run over as he ran. I also adored the time I borrowed a Chihuahua and dressed as Santa the stories that went around about how small Santa and Rudolph were tickled my funny bone for weeks. A whole new myth and legend ran rife around the forests and hills. No dog was safe as the cleverer kids tried to make their own adventure and attempted to fly, many a creature was run ragged. I was always waiting for said kids as some of them are very tasty. These days the visitors chasing the unreachable pot of gold are less and less as they follow the same dream by purchasing a lotto ticket.

All hoping for the same goal but the government is leading them in the dance, not me.

Although solitude is my preferred condition. The tourist board pays me to show myself every now and then. There would be a lot fewer visitors to our fabulous lush and green isle especially the Yankees if they didn't believe they had the opportunity myself to espy. I also have to leak some of my gold now and again but the aforementioned tourist board has the good grace to keep it topped up along with me aul pints of Guinness. Yep, I'm definitely living the life of Reilly as they say, and my naughty side adds the O. Yep it was plain Reilly until every time the boss heard of my antics he nearly always said Oh. So they called my Patrick O'Reilly eventually. I quite like the O it gives me a certain ring. I have oft thought about finding a Mrs O'Reilly when the head is immersed in Guinness but wake up the next morning green and as mentioned before that colour does not look good on me and I soon recover my senses when I look in the mirror.

Ah, I see a fresh batch of gobshites. I don't need a calendar there all clad in various shades of green Paddy's Day must be arriving. Jaysus time for me to get busy, when Spring is sprung my leisure time on the shelf is hung. I'll leave you with good aul Irish saying -

"May the Irish hills caress you. May her lakes and rivers bless you. May the luck of the Irish enfold you. May the blessings of Saint Patrick behold you."

Obsessed

It was an average day when I met him but my reaction to him was anything but average. I was completely and utterly besotted. When he smiled everything inside me went all gooey. Anything that had nothing to do with him was of no interest to me anymore.

I had held hands with boys before but he was the first of the male species that I knew I wanted more with. I was thirteen and should have been locked up, isolated for my own protection, but my mum didn't have the balls to confront me.

I used to happily go out in my school uniform and not care who saw me in it. Now as soon as I got in it was straight out of it and into what I considered to be cooler clothes. I started willingly doing extra jobs for mum just so I could get some extra money for clothes and some makeup.

The first time I lost my virginity was on a walk down to the waterfall. We used to hang out there, giggling and holding hands, sneaking kisses when no one was looking, because he was nineteen, at least that's what he told me. My friend, who hated him, told me he looked older. He said she was just fat and jealous. Leading up to the big event I saw less and less of her, until the only time I saw her was in school.

This day we actually went down to the water and took off our shoes and paddled. It was freezing and we huddled together for some warmth. He started tickling me and we both fell in the water. Drenched, I said my mum would kill me, he said no she won't we can take them off hang them off a branch and lay on the grass and talk until they're dry.

It seems like a good solution and for once I didn't resist when he started taking my clothes off. I took them off myself. Everything felt good, the kissing, the hand down there until he put it inside me. That hurt a bit, but he carried on. I don't think it lasted long but it seemed like an eternity at the time. Afterwards, he was so gentle and told me it would better the next time, that no girl liked their first time. He bought me back to the water and washed me down there. I was surprised to see blood on his hands. Is that normal? I had no one else to ask. I certainly wasn't going to ask my mum.

I began to enjoy it over time and it was worth it to make him happy. I finally had to introduce him to my mum because she just kept at me about where I was going and who was I seeing. I brought him for dinner one evening after school. He was his most charming self and I could tell she was taken with him even though she disapproved of the age gap.

She sat me down when he was gone and told me she was sending me to stay with aunt Jane for a while. I told there was no way in hell I was going and she couldn't make me. There was an almighty row and we came to blows. She'd often hit me before but this time I hit back. The shock on her face elated me. It drove me to hit her again and again until I couldn't stop. Luckily for me, it was the weekend and nobody would be looking for me or her. I called him and he came over, he didn't seem too bothered about the bloody mess he found on the floor. My Home Economics scissors embedded in my mother's neck.

He calmly told me we were going to make it look like a burglary that I walked in on.

He asked me to show him where my mum kept her good jewellery and upended the box on the floor before putting the jewellery in his pocket. He rifled through tea caddies finding hidden stashes I didn't even know about.

The police came but didn't believe by burglary story. I told them it was Joe and the bruises on my face on arms I said were caused by him. They preferred to believe that than think it was my mum. He got arrested and despite all his protestations of innocence was send down for seven years, he was on fact sixteen, not nineteen, that surprised me. I'm assuming his age was their reason for leniency.

I never went back to school, told everyone I was too traumatized by it all. I sit here now rubbing my stomach, smiling, knowing I'm going to be a great mum.

The stolen hearts Club

The stolen hearts formed a club. Each wanting to make a return to its original owner. The longer they resided outside a human body the smellier they got, so there was always a chance if they found them, they would be rejected. Once a week they picked an unsuspecting body loosened its heartstrings and squashed in. When his body burst as they always eventually do there is only so much heart one body can hold, and often, one of two of the stolen hearts get broken in the process. Hiding under the last one's coat they await their next hopefully temporary home.

Loves Bite

Lush fields flowers blooming the scent of spring in the air. I'm walking barefoot, devil-may-care. Hoping that I'll catch a glimpse of her, the one who haunts my every waking moment and dreams, hard to explain how gorgeous she is.

Hair as black as the darkest night and eyes grey like two slivers of the moon, curtained by the longest lashes, silken sashes. I had been told to stay away, rumours of black magic abound, but I aspire to tame her.

I hear a muffled scream in the distance someone has someone pinned and seems intent on having their wicked way. As I get closer I realise it's her and she is the aggressor, not the victim. Blood is dripping down her chin, and she gives me a satisfied grin as she proceeds to pick his skin from her teeth.

I acted all floppy and subservient and fell at her feet she looked at me like I was a piece of meat. As she bent for the kill I chopped at will. I had been hoping to get head of a different kind, but one takes what one can, the axe did a nice clean cut, surprisingly, she'll make a nice trophy.

The End

Don't miss out!

Visit the website below and you can sign up to receive emails whenever Susan O'Reilly publishes a new book. There's no charge and no obligation.

https://books2read.com/r/B-A-KVVW-MTZFC

BOOKS 2 READ

Connecting independent readers to independent writers.

Also by Susan O'Reilly

Changes Come
Snapshots
The Sound of Silence
Obsession a Novella Extended to Novel
Flash Horror